Hank
BECOMES A BIG
Brother

by Cissie Stevens

ISBN-13:978-1729044384

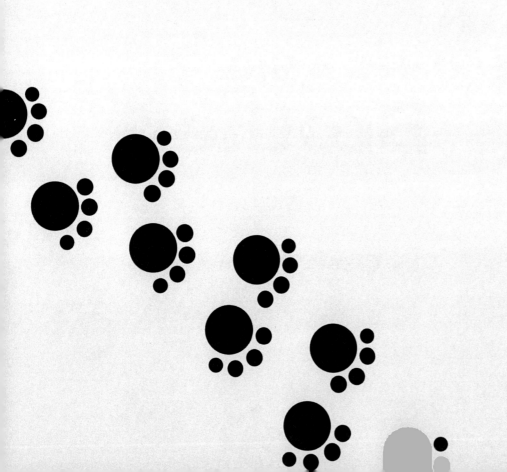

This book is dedicated to all the big brothers and sisters out there, and the little ones too!

H&B Productions
San Francisco, CA 94105
www.adventuresofhankandthebear.com

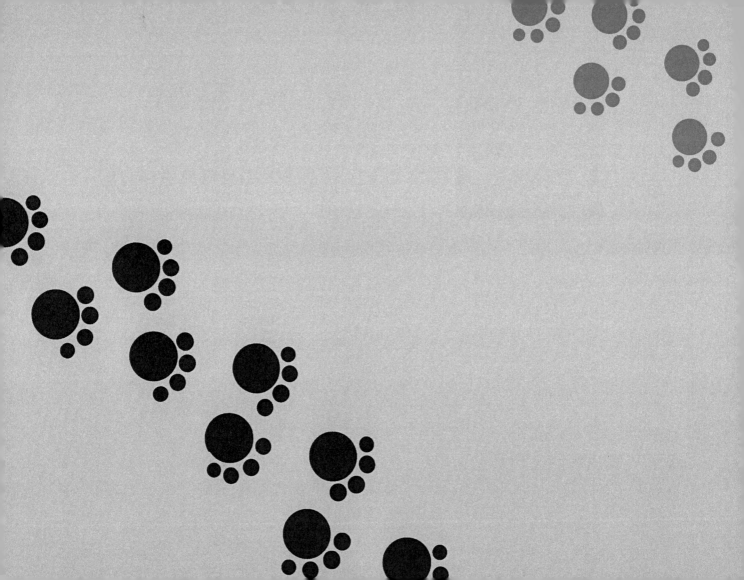

What is happening today?

Your little brother arrives today.

MY BROTHER?!
I can't wait!

Well, before
he gets here,
there is a lot to do.

Let's start by making a list. What do you think your brother will need?

THINGS FOR BROTHER

1.
2.
3.
4.
5.
6.
7.
8.
9.
10.

Help Hank with his list! What do you think Hank's brother will need? Write them on the notepad!

THINGS FOR BROTHER

1. Bottle
2. Dog Bed
3. Bowl + Food
4. Dog Toys
5. Xoxoto
6. Collar
7. Leash
8. ay Brush
9. Treats

What do you share with your brothers, sisters and friends? Write or draw the items below!

Dolls.

It means you and your brother can both play with the toys.

Yes! I can share my toys!

Okay, go pick out some toys to share with your brother.

Hmmm, he will probably want to play with these balls.

Oh! and this stuffed animal!

Can he sleep with me in my room?

That is a good idea, but I think you two will need a bigger bed. Let's update our list.

HANK'S ROOM

Okay, let's go to the store. When we get there, I am going to get his food, the treats and the new bed. Can you pick out three toys for him?

Yes Momma, I can pick out three toys for him!

For the second toy, a stuffed PIG! And for toy number three, a stick to chew on!

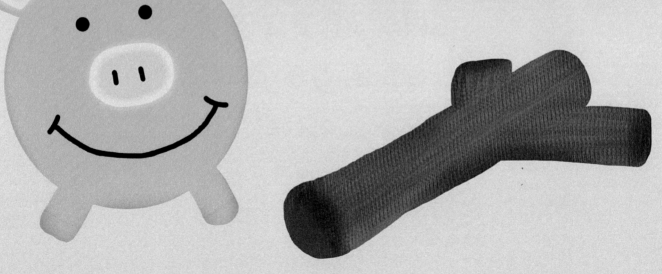

Momma, I got the toys!

Thank you Hank. I got the food, the treats and the new bed. Let's go back home and get the bedroom ready.

Momma, he's HERE!

This is so exciting! Let's open the door!

Bear, come inside and we can show you your bedroom.

We get to SHARE a room!

Look at all these toys!

Hank picked them out for you.

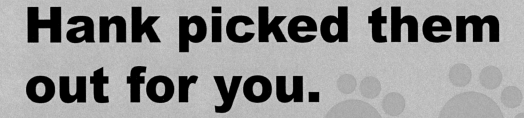

HANK and BEAR's ROOM

Thank you Hank! You are the best big brother. I love you and we are going to be best friends.

I am so happy you are part of our family. I love you too!

What are your favorite adventures?
Share them with us!

instagram @hankandthebear
www.facebook.com/hankandthebear